Today the town of Furryville's a very noisy place,
Crammed with crowds of creatures getting ready for a race.

The air is filled with honking horns and engines revving up,
As racers take their places for . . .

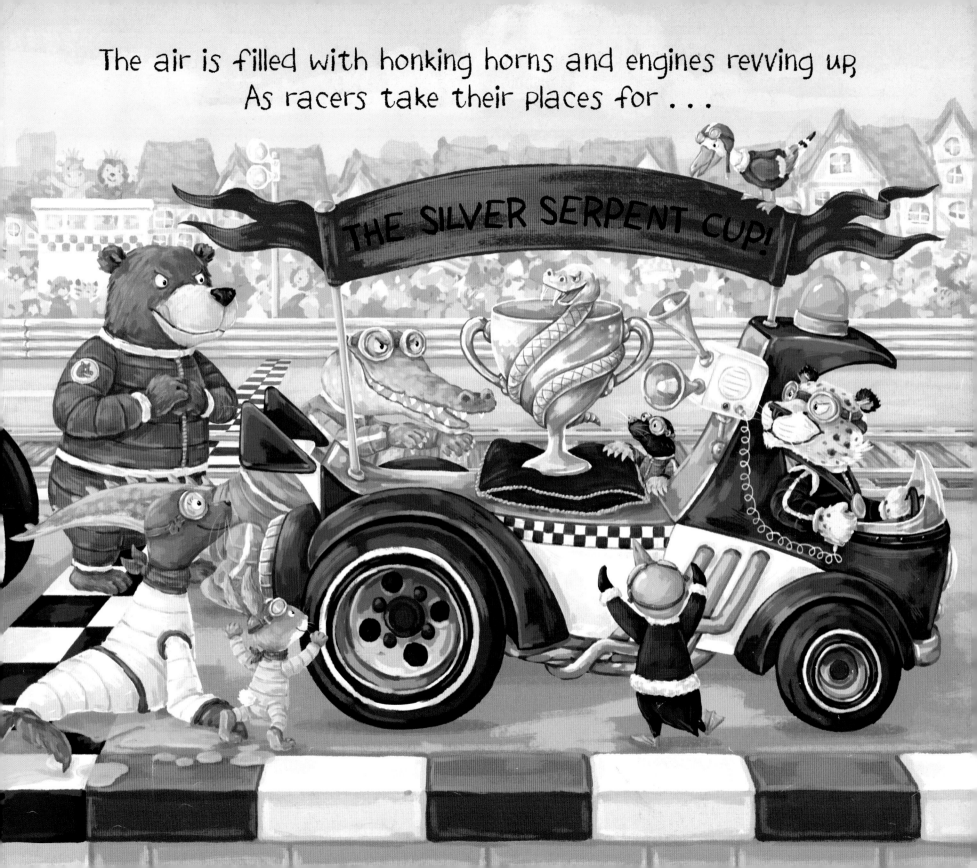

THE SILVER SERPENT CUP!

From Furryville to Featherport a thousand miles away,
This pack of eager animals will get there in one day.

On the ground or in the air, floating or submersed,
There's just one rule: to win this race you have to get there FIRST!

All kinds of different vehicles are lined up at the start.
Some are sleek and shiny . . .

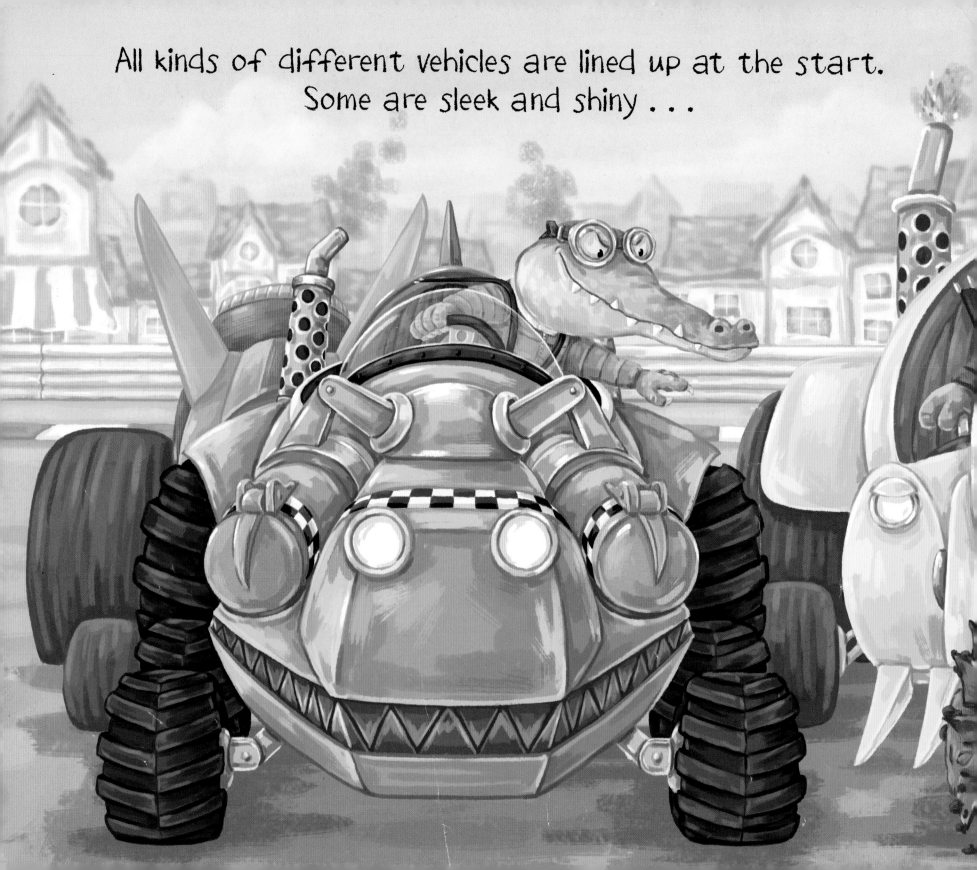

Everybody's ready,
so the race can now begin.

A siren sounds
and then
THEY'RE OFF
and may
the best
beast win!

and some
are not so
smart.

Of all the racers on the road the fastest one by far,
Is Roderick Von Rooster in his Hot Rod rocket car.

While all the other vehicles crowd together in a pack,
The Hot Rod fires its booster and then zooms off down the track.

Hurtling from the harbour and out across the bay,
Stephanie Skedaddle goes swiftly on her way.
Whooshing through the water in her sleek and stylish boat,
This seafaring sensation is the fastest thing afloat!

Creatures are competing UNDERNEATH the ocean too,
Where a shoal of submarines is bolting through the blue.

A shortcut through a shipwreck, carried out at breakneck speed,
Means that Ollie Octolinni has leapt into the lead.

We're halfway through the race now and on dry land again,
Where Baron Billy Blackstripes is racing in a train!

Spotting Roderick's Hot Rod on the highway up ahead,
Billy roars right past him and takes the lead instead.

The competition's getting fierce and high up in the sky,
Ella Egghart's aeroplane has just come soaring by.

As Featherport comes into view she has a beaky grin.
Everyone's behind her, so surely she must win.

But if you think it's over, well you'll have to think again,
As rockets fly across the sky and BLOW UP Ella's plane.

There's rockets flying everywhere. They're hitting everyone.
And blowing up their vehicles until all of them are gone!

Who fired all those rockets? Well the villain isn't far,
It's awful Al McNasty in his armoured aqua-car.

This ruthless, rotten reptile has a smug look on his face.
With all the other vehicles gone, he's bound to take first place.

Al's almost at the finish when he hears a rumbling sound,
And something big and pointy erupts OUT OF THE GROUND!
The rockets missed one racer who ran the race unseen,
And that was . . .

Max O'Moley in his tunnelling machine!

Max comes UP THROUGH the finish line to thunderous applause,
And swiftly snatches victory from Al's astonished jaws.
Of all the ways to win the race, Al's had to be the worst,
So everyone's delighted that Max has come in first!

Tonight the town of Featherport's a very noisy place,
As everybody celebrates a most momentous race.
And all the other animals whose vehicles were blown up
Cheer for Max the winner of . . .

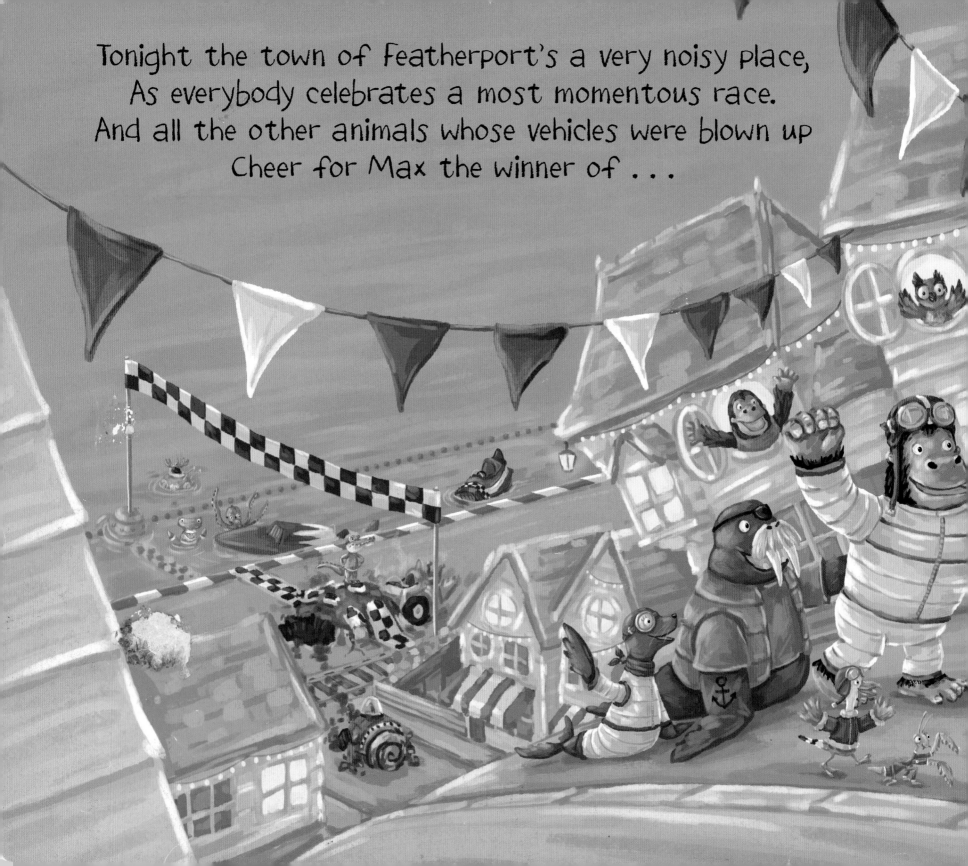

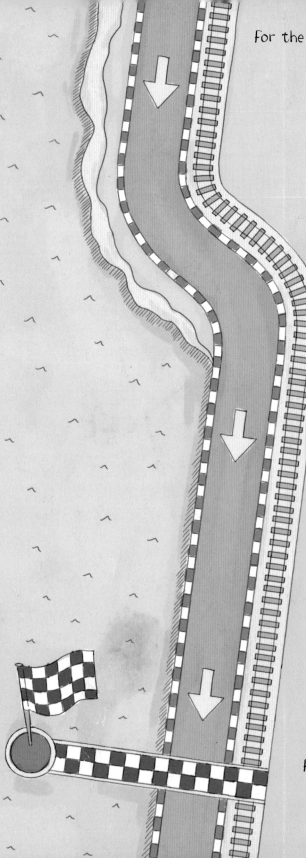

For the children of Asfordby Captain's Close Primary School. J.E.
For Theodore xx. E.E

OXFORD
UNIVERSITY PRESS

Great Clarendon Street, Oxford OX2 6DP

Oxford University Press is a department of the University of Oxford.
It furthers the University's objective of excellence in research, scholarship,
and education by publishing worldwide in

Oxford New York

Auckland Cape Town Dar es Salaam Hong Kong Karachi
Kuala Lumpur Madrid Melbourne Mexico City Nairobi
New Delhi Shanghai Taipei Toronto

With offices in
Argentina Austria Brazil Chile Czech Republic France Greece
Guatemala Hungary Italy Japan Poland Portugal Singapore
South Korea Switzerland Thailand Turkey Ukraine Vietnam

Text copyright © 2015 Jonathan Emmett
Illustration copyright © 2015 Ed Eaves

The moral rights of the author and artist have been asserted

Database right Oxford University Press (maker)

First published 2015

British Library Cataloguing in Publication Data available

ISBN: 978-0-19-273862-2 (paperback)
978-0-19-273863-9 (eBook)

10 9 8 7 6 5 4 3 2 1

Printed in China

Paper used in the production of this book is a natural, recyclable product made
from wood grown in sustainable forests. The manufacturing process conforms
to the environmental regulations of the country of origin

Find out more about Jonathan Emmett's books at
scribblestreet.co.uk

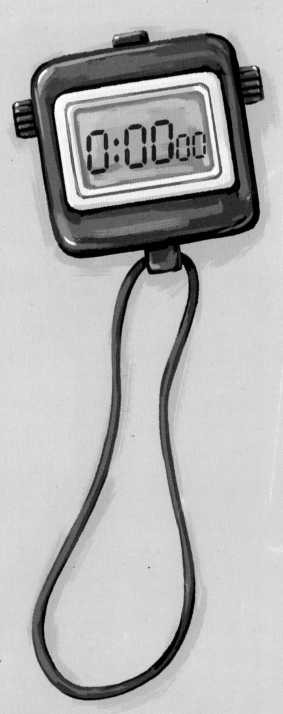

Bruce and Barney Battenberg

Burt Bourguignon

Hank 'The Hammer' Chompski

Bucky Hopkins

Doctor Waldo Snapper

Sir Hugo Hefflington

Salvador Squawky

Posy Pinkerton

Otto Von Skirmish

Sergeant Boris Blastovich

Gertrude Kerfuffle

Bess and Bonnie Bumblebutt